Dear Daisy, Get Well Soon

MAGGIE SMITH

CROWN PUBLISHERS, INC. ♛ NEW YORK

On Sunday,
my friend Daisy
came down with the chicken pox,
and she couldn't come out to play.

On Monday,
I made a card that said,
"Get Well Soon,"

and I sent it over...

...to Daisy.

On Tuesday,
I picked
two bunches of flowers,

and I sent them over...

...to Daisy.

On Wednesday,
I got down
three coloring books,

and I sent them over...

...to Daisy.

On Thursday,
I picked
four shiny apples,

and I sent them over…

...to Daisy.

On Friday,
I blew up
five rainbow balloons,

and I sent them over…

...to Daisy.

On Saturday,
I got a note that said,
"Please come over."

So I went on over...

...to Daisy's,

and we played all day.

For Peter, of course

Published by Crown Publishers, Inc., a Random House company,
201 East 50th Street, New York, New York 10022

CROWN and colophon are trademarks of Random House, Inc.
www.randomhouse.com/kids
Printed in Singapore

Library of Congress Cataloging-in-Publication Data
Smith, Maggie, 1965–
Dear Daisy, get well soon / Maggie Smith. — 1st ed.
p.   cm.
Summary: When his friend Daisy gets sick, Peter sends her more
gifts each day of the week until she feels better.
ISBN 0-517-80072-1 (trade). — 0-517-80073-X (lib. bdg.)
(1. Chicken pox—Fiction. 2. Days—Fiction. 3. Counting.)
I. Title.
PZ7.S65474Dg 2000   99-34058
(E)—dc21

10 9 8 7 6 5 4 3 2 1
April 2000
First Edition

16 95

n

Picture SMITH

Smith, Maggie, 1965–

Dear Daisy, get well soon